OTHER YEARLING BOOKS YOU WILL ENJOY:

YEARLING BOOKS/YOUNG YEARLINGS/YEARLING CLASSICS are designed especially to entertain and enlighten young people. Patricia Reilly Giff, consultant to this series, received her bachelor's degree from Marymount College. She holds a master's degree in history from St. John's University, and a Professional Diploma in Reading from Hofstra University. She was a teacher and reading consultant for many years, and is the author of numerous books for young readers.

For a complete listing of all Yearling titles, write to
Dell Readers Service, P.O. Box 1045,
South Holland, IL 60473.

The Secret Museum

by Sheila Greenwald

A Yearling Book

Published by
Dell Publishing
a division of
Bantam Doubleday Dell Publishing Group, Inc.
666 Fifth Avenue
New York, New York 10103

To Julius Greenwald

ISBN: 0-440-40148-8

Printed in the United States of America

March 1989

10 9 8 7 6 5 4 3 2 1

CW

I

Jennifer Fairfax sat at the kitchen table watching her mother roll out a ball of dough. The August afternoon sun filled the kitchen with a yellow light.

"What kind of pie will it be?" she asked.

"If you pick me some blackberries, it will be a blackberry pie," said her mother.

"How many shall I gather?" said Jennifer.

"If you fill this pot," said Mrs. Fairfax, taking a large pot off a hook on the wall, "we'll have a fat pie."

"If I can fill two pots, we'll have enough for jam," said Jennifer.

Jennifer's mother swung her long blond

ponytail over her shoulder and smiled. "Practical Jennifer," she said. "You can daydream the weeks away, but your ideas are always sensible. It is a gift and I don't know where you get it from." She pressed down on the dough. "Don't forget to put on your boots, honey. Those thorns can be mean."

Jennifer searched around the kitchen for her boots. The kitchen was actually set into one corner of a very large room which they called the studio. Filling one corner of the room was Jennifer's father's loom, his raw wool, and the bottles of vegetable dyes with which he colored the wool and cotton he used to create rugs and fabrics and wall hangings. The rest of the room served to exhibit his work as well as Jennifer's mother's pottery. Beatrice Fairfax was a potter. She worked in the barn where she had her potter's wheel and kiln.

The studio had been Jennifer's parents' dream for many years. They had planned for it and saved for it. When Jennifer's grandmother had left them the old house, where Jennifer's mother had herself grown up, they had thought their chance had come. They remodeled the house themselves, ripping down walls, exposing beams, setting in new windows to let in the view and the light. Finally they gave up their jobs as teachers in the city to move up to the country house and work at what they loved to do.

Unfortunately, they couldn't sell the work they loved to do. After the first six months of delight, they began to worry. They had put a beautiful sign out on the road:

BEATRICE AND HUGH FAIRFAX

CRAFTS, POTTERY, HAND-WOVEN RUGS

AND WALL HANGINGS

Hugh Fairfax, a tall red-haired man with a deep laugh, had painted the sign himself and hung it out on the road with great high hopes. At first he said that it always took a while before things got going: that this would be a year of difficulty which they'd all look back on and laugh about one day, and that nothing ever started with a bang. Beatrice Fairfax said they couldn't fail to make a go of it because their things were beautiful and sensibly priced, and it was merely a question of time till word got around. But then three months had passed and only a few cars had stopped. One family who had come in to ask directions stayed on to look at the work and bought a mug for two dollars. Somebody bought a rug and somebody else said they would but never came back.

The money from the rug was nearly gone, and Jennifer saw that worry had settled in their house like a sad unwelcome guest. "The summer will be better," her father had said in the spring. But now summer was half over and it had not been better. It seemed the house was full of her mother's unsold pottery and her father's fabrics. The sight of them, beautiful as they were, became a depressing reminder of how the summer had not been better.

That morning at breakfast Hugh Fairfax had said, "We could move back to the city and see if we can get our old jobs back."

"Let's give it the rest of the summer before we decide," said Beatrice Fairfax. "Maybe things will get better in August."

Jennifer found her boots and put them on. It

was good to think of blackberries and pies and forget about the worries. With the pots in her hands, she set out on that fine afternoon in the first week of August to discover things that had happened in no daydream she had ever had and which would make this the most unusual summer any of the Fairfaxes had known.

2

The Fairfaxes lived in the rolling hilly farm country of the Hudson valley in New York State. From the top of the hill behind their barn, Jennifer could see the silos of two large dairy farms, the rushing clear water of a small river, and the mysterious peaks and turrets of the house they called the Mansion. The few younger children on the road liked to pretend that the Mansion was haunted. Actually, the huge old house was simply closed. Some of its gardens were still kept up by a gardener, because Mrs. Needham, who owned the Mansion (though she rarely visited it), could not bear to think of it turning into a complete ruin.

Jennifer's mother could remember the time

many years before when the Needhams had filled their mansion with life. There had been tennis courts and formal gardens, goldfish ponds, an aviary, a garden for rare flowers and one for rosebushes. Three gardeners had worked full time tending the Needhams' gardens, fifteen maids tended the Needhams' house, and four men tended their cars and boats and guests and whatever else needed tending. Jennifer knew all this because her mother had been called in to work at the Needhams' when they had so many guests that extra help was required.

"But that was a long time ago," Mrs. Fairfax liked to say. "I was a very young girl. Mr. Needham was a lovely man. I don't know why his wife closed the house up after he died. She couldn't bring herself to sell it, and she couldn't bring herself to use it without him." Mrs. Needham lived in the city and the Mansion stood empty.

There were no other children Jennifer's age on the road, but she didn't mind being alone, because she loved to go down to the Mansion to walk and think and make it her own place. The turnoff to the Mansion road was not far from her own house. The stone gatehouse to the side of the Mansion road was empty. Just beyond the gatehouse the road turned, and as one rounded the curve, the main house suddenly appeared. The house was still grand and beautiful, even after twenty-five years of neglect.

Past the main house lay what had been a formal garden where once hedges had been clipped to resemble birds and boxes and cones. A pond and waterfall were beyond the garden and then the road forked. One branch went down to a lake, the other to what had been a tennis court. On either side of the road to the lake were masses of the best blackberry bushes in the county. It was to those bushes that Jennifer went with two pots in her hands, her boots on her feet, and thoughts of pies and jam.

The berries were growing thick and fat. They glistened bluey black. She hardly had to tap them and they fell into her pot with a heavy plop. Everything around her smelled strongly of the juices plants put out at the middle of summer. Jennifer emptied branches at the bottom where the berries were most plump and, trying to avoid the thorns, looked under and over to see where the next good bush would be. She turned this way and that and followed an overgrown path, covered with foxglove and chicory, to still another overgrown path and another good bush.

Her pots were full, a mosquito buzzed at her ear, her arms stung where thorns had scratched them, a crow cawed. She was ready to go home. She looked around her and knew she was lost. The path went three different ways. The three different ways all looked alike. She didn't know which to follow. Her heart began to thump. She decided to try one of the paths, and if that didn't work, another. Then the sound of someone crying surprised her out of her plan.

Jennifer followed the sound into a mass of leafy underbrush, almost too thick to pass through. The crying was getting closer. It was the saddest sound she had ever heard. She managed to get through the underbrush and could see that just beyond it there was a clearing. She emerged from the viny tangle of branches into a field of high grass.

In the center of the field was a small house. The house was exactly like the Mansion. It was even a ruin like the big house. It had every terrace and column and portico, only it was the size of a cabin.

The sound of crying stopped as Jennifer stared in astonishment at the little house. Still clutching her blackberry pots, she slowly walked up to it. The wood of the front steps had rotted and she had to walk carefully lest she fall through. There was a sudden rustling sound and then a beating of wings. A small brown bird flew out of a broken window.

When she touched the door, it swung open, falling back on its hinges as if it had been waiting for the chance. Jennifer stepped into a misty room, filled with the light of late afternoon, and gazed on the strangest sight she had ever seen.

3

A long low table extended the length of the room. Seated around the table were at least twenty dolls. They were of different sizes and types, but every doll wore an expression of such misery and was in such a state of dirty neglect that they all looked alike. At the head of the table, cobwebs dangling from their crowns, were a pair of King and Queen dolls. They were tilted in their chairs, as if bowed down by the weight of the dust on them.

Jennifer approached the table. She saw small china cups for tea, she saw plates for cakes, she saw a small teapot with matching sugar bowl and creamer, and in the middle of it all sat a bird's nest made of twigs and mud and speckled with feathers.

She circled the table, and when she reached the Queen doll's chair she put down her pots of berries and, taking the doll in both hands, propped her up on her chair. It was then she noticed what she thought was a drop of water coursing down the doll's waxy cheek, leaving a muddy track.

Surely it was a spot of dew, Jennifer thought, for she was a sensible girl and knew that dolls did not weep. But when she wiped away the drop another followed after it, leaving another track from eye to chin. Jennifer looked into the round blue circles of the doll's eyes, which in most dolls bear a staring fixed expression. She saw to her surprise a look of clouded sadness.

All this was so odd that Jennifer drew back and looked out of the window, saying aloud to herself as she did so, "This is not really happening; it is not possible for dolls to cry." She shut her eyes tight and counted to ten and then repeated, "Dolls don't cry." She opened her eyes slowly, turned around slowly, looked at the

doll, and saw the tear still damp on the doll's
cheek.

Jennifer picked up her pots of berries and firmly walked to the door. She stood out on the small rotting porch for a few minutes, proving to herself that she was not in the middle of a dream by pinching her arm, stamping her foot, and whistling. Then she tried to think up sensible reasons for water to appear on the doll's cheek. "A leak in the ceiling," she said aloud. "But it isn't raining." Melting wax? But why just from the eye?

Finally she went back inside to find out the truth, however impossible or strange or simple it might be. She approached the Queen doll slowly, frowning with concentration. She studied the miserable little wax face. Sure enough, another single tear had begun to form. Jennifer found she was curiously moved by the doll's sad expression.

"You poor wretched thing," she said softly, smoothing the Queen doll's hair back from her brow. The hair was surprisingly fine and silky to touch. "How on earth did you get to be in this awful state?"

Jennifer's question was, of course, idle. She was used to talking to herself on her long walks, but she wasn't expecting a response and was startled when a creaky sound followed her question. She looked out the window and around the room, for she felt the sound had been close by, and then she heard it again. It was a sad and lonely sound, like that of a shutter stirred by the wind. Jennifer grasped the table and once again the rusty creak was repeated. It had become a word. The word was "Woe."

Jennifer studied the still sad faces one by one, her amazement increasing. Her eyes came to the King doll. His lips were slightly parted, his gaze met hers.

"Woe," he creaked again, trying, it seemed, to shake the dust off his voice. "Woe to us."

Jennifer clapped her hand over her own lips to silence a cry of astonishment.

"Woe to us," the voice repeated. Each word was as deep and sad as the sound of weeping Jennifer had followed just a few minutes before. "Nobody has wiped her cheek for years. She was so lovely once. She gave such pleasure. We all did."

"But she's still lovely," said Jennifer quickly, determined not to show her amazement.

"What difference does it make?" said the Queen, parting her sooty lips. "No one cares. We sit here through years and days. We feel our clothes turn stiff with age and crack with dust. We tip in our chairs and no one straightens us up. Where are the children? Where did the children go? Once there were children."

"We were taken out and played with every day," said a Russian Peasant doll at the other end of the table.

"Dressed and undressed," said a Princess doll.

"Washed and dried," said a dimpled Baby doll.

"Abandoned and forgotten now," said a Jester doll.

"What's the use?" said the Queen.

"No use," said the King.

"Nonsense," said Jennifer. "I'm here. I'm a

child. I'll wash you and dress you and polish you up. That's all you need. Soap and water."

"No use," said the King.

Jennifer realized that the dolls had been sitting in this hopeless silent manner for years, and though they hardly seemed to notice her presence, her arrival had set them off. She understood this because since her parents began to worry they had noticed less and less of what went on around them, so preoccupied were they by their thoughts. All they needed was a listening ear to start them talking.

"All children do is forget you," said the Queen. "Drag you here and there and nearly break your head, and then one day they're out the door and it's as if you never existed. Only the bird cares now."

"And I have the most beautiful head," said the King. "Sculpted like a statue. Have you noticed the workmanship on my nose?"

"You've only pointed it out seven thousand nine hundred and twenty-five times," said the Queen in a tone which Jennifer thought stated it more as a matter of fact than to hurt his feelings.

"That makes it seven thousand nine hundred and twenty-six times," said the King.

"If you're looking for workmanship," said the Jester, "I think you'd best consider my eyes. They are very unusual for a doll, you know. Most dolls have these round stupid blue marble things. Not me. Dark brown, piercing, and intelligent they are. Take a good look."

All the blue-eyed dolls seemed to turn just a fraction of an inch away from the Jester doll in annoyance.

"You are all very vain," said Jennifer, who had just learned the word and thought the dolls a perfect example of it.

"Of course we're vain," said the Queen, addressing Jennifer for the first time. "What do you expect a doll to be? Look at the girl, your Highness," she said to the King.

All the dolls directed their round staring gaze at Jennifer.

"Why should I look at the girl?" said the

King haughtily. "Who invited her? We're not exactly ready for company."

"All you need is a good washing," said Jennifer, and then to her surprise she added, "I'm just sick and tired of listening to you complain."

"Tut tut tut," said the little Princess doll. "Whoever asked you, anyway?"

The other dolls joined her, making a chorus of "Whoever asked you, anyway?"

As they cackled and tittered in a mechanical rusty way, Jennifer picked up her pots of blackberries and walked to the rickety door. They were such a strange and proud collection that instead of being offended by them, she was touched.

"Why did you speak to me?" she said softly.

The Queen doll grew very serious. "We did you an honor," she said. "We have never spoken before, and we may never again. We spoke because we have been silent for so long and because someone had to be told of our misery."

"Is this really happening?" said Jennifer.

"Perhaps not," said the Queen. "If you don't come back you'll never know."

"And if I do come back?" said Jennifer.

"You still may never know," the Queen said.

Standing on the broken porch of the little house, Jennifer realized that the sun was going down over one of the paths. Her own house always seemed to be where the sun was going down if you started from the Needhams' land. As she began to follow the path that went toward the sun, she noticed the small brown bird darting from tree to porch, back to tree, back to porch, and then through the window back into the house.

4

Jennifer knew from the first moment she woke up the next morning that as soon as she could, she was going to the old playhouse. Having this plan made the morning seem different. The air seemed clearer, the colors of her father's rugs brighter. Her mother's jugs filled with wild flowers and the hanging pots for ferns and spider plants looked fresh and beautiful.

"My goodness, just look at this girl," said her mother at breakfast. "What energy. I wish I had some of it. The sight of fifty unsold sugar bowls and twenty unsold vases and thirty-nine unsold mugs, not to mention seven salad bowls, doesn't make me feel like getting to work."

"Why don't you rent a shop?" said Jennifer through a mouthful of granola. She had always wondered how on earth her parents hoped to sell anything from a country road with only one sign to tell they were there, and that sign usually blocked by trees. Hugh and Beatrice Fairfax exchanged glances.

"Because that costs money," said Beatrice Fairfax, turning her head away as if to close the conversation.

"How much?" Jennifer persisted.

"More than we have, because we don't have any," her mother said. Then she seemed to change her mind about something, for she turned and reached across the table and took Jennifer's hand. "I'm sorry I just snapped at you, Jenny," she said. "You can't know about things we haven't explained to you, so let me tell you the situation. We thought we could make this work out up here, and we've really tried to make it work."

"We had to spend a lot of time and all our

savings fixing the place up," her father said. "In order to buy equipment and materials we borrowed money on the house from the bank. That's called a mortgage. We have to pay the bank back every month."

"We thought we'd make the money to pay the bank by selling our work," said Jennifer's mother, "and so we got busy, as you know, and did a great deal. We realized that things would be slow at the start, but we never dreamed they'd be this slow."

"We've tried everything we can think of to make this place work out," Hugh Fairfax said, "but we can't do things we haven't thought of." He had been smiling; now he sighed. "We've run out of ideas and money. So if you've got any really terrific notions, Jenny, don't keep them to yourself."

"I won't," Jennifer said. "Thanks for telling me things."

Though her parents had talked to her honestly, Jenny could not bring herself to tell them about the dolls. She loved the idea of having a secret place, as private as the designs on her father's loom or the shapes of her mother's pottery. The playhouse was her hidden place of dreams. She didn't want to share with it anyone yet.

When she finished breakfast, Jennifer put on her boots and took two pots, along with a bottle of water, soap, and a sponge. She had no trouble finding the playhouse. She saw where she had trampled the bushes the day before. The house was exactly as she had seen it last, which surprised her, since she almost thought she'd dreamed it. As she climbed onto the porch the brown bird flew out of the broken window again.

The dolls were just as forlorn as they had been. The bright morning light made them appear even dirtier.

"Hello," said Jennifer, standing at the door. The dolls stared at her. "Now then, who is going to be first?" She set the pots on the floor and filled them with water from the bottle. "You," she pointed to the Queen doll, "you should be first."

"Not I," said the Queen. "I am too digni-
fied."

"Then who?" said Jennifer. "One of you
must."

She looked down the table of assorted baby
dolls, lady dolls, and gentleman dolls.

"Very well," said the Jester. "If it doesn't

work out, I'll just look more comical, and that's the point of me, isn't it?"

Jennifer picked him up very carefully. She soaped her sponge and with delicate strokes wiped his face. The sponge left his waxy forehead a glowing pink. His face looked good as new after a few more wipes. He was a wonderfully made doll. The other dolls' eyes seemed to enlarge as they stared at him. Carefully Jennifer rubbed his velvet jacket and pants with the damp sponge till all the lint and dust were off. Then she wiped his wax hands and wooden feet. All the while she worked, nineteen pairs of blue and one pair of brown round eyes watched in silence. After she'd cleaned the Jester she sat him back in his chair.

"Aren't you nice," said the Russian Peasant doll. "You look the way you used to, Jester. All new and shiny."

The Jester seemed to brighten a shade more.

"Could you do me next?" said the Peasant doll.

"Royalty comes first," said the Queen doll.

"Those who ask first come first," said Jennifer.

"Then royalty comes second," said the Queen.

Jennifer washed the Peasant and her cotton dress and then the Queen. The Princess and the King came after that. Since their clothes were silk, Jennifer shook the dust off them but feared a washing would ruin the old material. Then she simply started around the table, washing and sponging till the water in the pots was black and she had to go down to the Needhams' lake for fresh water.

She made the trip down to the lake four times that day. The small brown bird darted behind and in front of her on the path.

Jennifer's arms and fingers were stiff from sponging and wringing and fetching. It seemed as if no time at all had passed when she noticed the sun coming at a slant through the window, and the light was the rich yellow of late afternoon. Jennifer was very hungry. She looked at the table. Twenty bright faces met her gaze,

34

clean and beautiful. They were extraordinary-looking dolls. The King was right; they were sculpted and molded with great artistry.

Jennifer brought the damp cotton clothes in and spread them over the backs of the chairs. Then she put on her boots and gathered the pots and sponge and soap. Just before she left, she picked up the bird's nest very carefully from the table and carried it with her to the door.

"Don't destroy the bird's nest," the King said. "She is our friend. She was hatched here and so returns every year. Set it down someplace where she'll be happy. Someplace near."

"I will," said Jennifer.

The King coughed. "And please don't forget us."

"I won't," said Jennifer.

5

Jennifer placed the nest on a low network of branches where she thought it would balance without falling.

When she returned home she found Beatrice and Hugh Fairfax sitting out on the small lawn in front of the barn. She could sense their worry before she could hear them speaking. Her father's head was down on his hand. He was lost in thought. Her mother's chin rested on her fist and she was speaking in a low serious voice.

"Hi, Jenny," her father said when he saw her, and he smiled. "How's our girl? Where have you been?"

"What's up?" said Jennifer.

"We just got our bank statement, honey," said her mother, "and the news isn't very good."

"How bad is it?" said Jennifer.

"Bad enough," said Hugh Fairfax. Then he

tried to smile again. "Let's look at it this way. We tried something that we always wanted to do and it didn't work, but at least we tried it. So when we go back to the city we'll know what it was like to do this thing. That's very important. We'll have had our chance."

"But I don't want to go back," said Jennifer. "I like it up here."

"You do?" said her mother. "You seem very lonely. There aren't any children your age around, and you didn't find many friends at the school."

"But I liked the school," said Jennifer, "and I don't need lots of friends around." The city seemed so far away to her now, so large and noisy and crowded. It was very hard to think of going back, especially since she'd found the dolls. "You haven't tried everything," she blurted. "You haven't tried a store."

"It's not that easy to sell things from a store," said her mother. "The store has to want to sell them."

"Then put up a new sign," said Jennifer angrily. "The old one has a branch in front of it."

Hugh Fairfax pulled Jennifer to him and hugged her. "You know something," he said. "The girl is right, Bea. We haven't done very much with publicity. We need some new and good ideas."

"I know something else we need," said Beatrice Fairfax.

"What's that?" said Jennifer.

"Luck," said her mother. "Good luck, not the sort we've had till now."

They went in to get dinner ready, but Jennifer couldn't think up any other ideas for publicity. Instead she decided to ask her mother some of the questions she'd wondered about ever since she found the dolls. Whose were they? Were they antiques?

"Did Mrs. Needham have any children?" she said as they set the table.

"No," said her mother, "why do you ask?"

"I found an old doll lying around and I wondered whose it was."

Beatrice Fairfax put a large salad on the table

while her husband served out the chili. She sat down and picked up her fork. She had the dreamy look she got when she talked about growing up on the road, before she went off to art school. "I heard a story once that there was an old doll house hidden away in a secret place and it was full of rare and beautiful antique dolls. Mrs. Lane, the Needhams' cook, told me that, but I never knew whether to believe the things she said, and I haven't seen her since she moved into town. She told me Mrs. Needham's grandfather built the doll house to look just like the Mansion and filled it with beautiful dolls. But I would think she'd have taken them out long ago if they were that important. Certainly she wouldn't have left one lying around for you to find, Jennifer. You must have found somebody else's old doll."

Jennifer thought she would have to handle the dolls very carefully when she played with them. They were more valuable than she had imagined.

6

Jennifer was glad to leave the house the next morning. Her parents were trying very hard to keep their spirits up, but beneath their smiles was the worry they had talked of the night before.

She had taken with her a mop, some dust rags, a can of furniture polish, and a bucket. Just before she turned down the Needhams' road a loud voice called, "Hey there, Miss Jennifer, are you off to tidy up the Mansion?"

Jennifer whirled around to see elderly Mrs. McBride leaning over her fence, smiling broadly. She had been a good friend of Jennifer's grandmother and had known Jennifer's mother when she was a little girl.

"You look like a soldier marching along with that mop," said Mrs. McBride. "I wish your granny was alive to see you." Mrs. McBride had once worked as housekeeper for Mrs. Needham and lived on at the housekeeper's cottage. Her husband, who sat in a rocker on the porch, had been head gardener for the Needhams, before arthritis crippled him. He waved to Jennifer.

"How's your Ma?" he said.

"Just fine," said Jennifer.

"Where you off to?"

"I just wanted to play house in the woods," Jennifer said.

"I'll pay you fifteen cents an hour if you take my granddaughter, Miss Lizzie the Terrible McBride, with you. She's bored to death and driving me nutty," said Mrs. McBride.

"I can't," said Jennifer quickly.

"Can't?" Mrs. McBride's brows lifted with surprise. "Why, I'd think you'd jump at the chance, especially since I know you don't get a cent allowance."

"Any other time I'd love to babysit her," said Jennifer, "but just not today."

"BABYSIT ME?" a voice screeched from the screen porch. The screen door slammed and a girl jumped off the porch. Her face was dark with rage. "I don't need any babysitters," she bellowed. "I could babysit her." She glared down at Jennifer through dirty horn-rimmed glasses. "I happen to be ten years and six months old."

"Then act it," said her grandmother coolly. "And stop tearing around here like some two-year-old juvenile delinquent."

"There isn't anything to do," said Lizzie. "The place is half-dead. No toys, no kids, nothing. I wish I was home instead of this miserable dump." She crossed her arms over her chest and scowled at Jennifer.

Jennifer stared back at her. Lizzie had the city-white skin that she herself had always had, red hair tied in pigtails, and very mean blue eyes.

"Jennifer Fairfax came up here from the city

43

only six months ago," Mrs. McBride said calmly, "and I didn't hear any complaints out of her. She seems to find lots of things to do with herself."

"Well, lucky for lucky old her," Lizzie yelled, and made a hideous face at Jennifer. "Now get lost."

"Good-bye," Jennifer said, and ran off down the Needhams' road, never looking back.

As she approached the playhouse, no bird flew out of the broken window. Jennifer set to work immediately. She dusted and polished the room and its furniture. She filled her bucket from the lake and washed out the tea set. She shined the table and the chairs and set them straight. Then, trying not to tear the delicate fabrics, she carefully dressed the dolls.

Finally everything was done. The clean dolls in their clean clothes sat straight up on dusted chairs around a gleaming table set with porcelain teacups and cake dishes. Jennifer stood back to admire what she had done. She was tired and hot and pleased with herself. She thought of the cool lake. "I'll be back soon," she said to the dolls, and closed the door behind her.

She ran off, following the path to the lake.

The small brown bird darted over her head, settling first on one bush and then another, only to soar up as she approached.

At the lake Jennifer slipped out of her jeans and shirt and waded into the water, letting the biting coolness surround her. She floated on her back and splashed and swished around a few times, doing what she thought of as a water ballet. Then she lay on her back and looked at the sky and the purple stalks of loosestrife that ringed the lake.

The sun went behind a cloud and the air turned surprisingly chill. The brown bird suddenly flew out of some bushes and darted over the lake, circling over Jennifer, chirping frantically. Jennifer was alarmed. She felt the bird was trying to give her a message. She hurried out of the water and mopped herself off with the dish towel before getting back into her clothes. She ran down the path to the house, the bird chirping and shrilling in front of her. When she saw the house her feeling of alarm grew, for the door was wide open.

7

Everything was ruined. The dolls were heaped and tossed on the table and in the corners. Their clothes were flung every which way. Their hair was in a tangle. Jennifer fell on her knees and started to pick the dolls up one by one. Their faces were smudged and miserable.

"Someone came," said the Queen doll. "We thought she came to play with us, now that we're so lovely. But she knocked us down and toppled the chairs."

"No real harm seems to have been done," Jennifer said with relief. Things looked worse than they were.

She set to work again. She tidied the room and straightened the dolls and wiped their faces and combed their hair and didn't stop working until they looked as they had before, except for one difference. Their faces wore a curious fearful expression.

"Don't worry," said Jennifer as she was leaving. "I'll be back early in the morning."

"We will worry," said the Peasant doll. "Somebody else knows about us, and she is cruel."

Jennifer didn't say anything to the dolls, but she certainly had an excellent idea who the somebody else was. What to do about Lizzie McBride was the problem she had to put her mind to.

It was a long night for Jennifer. She hardly ate any supper, slept little, and had no breakfast in the morning. She ran all the way to the playhouse, sure that disaster had struck again. She thought she saw someone move behind a tangle of bushes, but when she poked around in them she found nothing. Finally she opened

the door to the house. The dolls were as she had left them.

"I think," said the Queen very grandly, "that some sort of celebration is in order."

"Why's that?" said the King.

"To honor our restoration," said the Queen.

"That's two celebrations then," said Jester. "We've been restored twice."

"Very funny," said the Queen without laughing.

"If that other one keeps coming we'll have to be restored and restored," the Jester persisted.

The Queen shuddered. "May she never come again."

"What sort of celebration did you have in mind, my dear?" said the King.

"Why, a ball!" the Queen cried. "A real ball with dancing and singing and elegant games and buttercup cake and dandelion tea and clover wine."

Jennifer moved the table and chairs to the side of the room. Then she went out and picked buttercups and dandelions and clover. She arranged the buttercup petals on plates. She stirred the dandelions into water and mixed the clover blossoms into the teacups. Then she put the dolls together into dancing couples and, singing the music herself, she whirled them around the floor until she was breathless.

"Oh, charming, charming," cried the Princess to the Jester. "You're as nimble and graceful as ever. I could fall in love with you."

"Then do so," said the Jester. "Do so."

When they were all exhausted, Jennifer put them back on their chairs.

She was preparing to serve the clover wine when she felt the door behind her open and saw the expression of horror in the eyes of the watching dolls.

8

Lizzie McBride stood on the threshold. She was completely still except for her mouth, which chewed vigorously on a big pink wad of bubble gum.

"What do you want?" said Jennifer.

"I'm just looking around," said Lizzie. "Nice little place you got here. Your folks give it to you?"

"Nobody gave it to me," said Jennifer. "How did you get here?"

"I followed you," said Lizzie.

"Did you follow me yesterday, too?"

"What if I did?" Lizzie blew a big bubble which popped and covered the end of her nose like a stocking.

"If you did, then you're the one who messed up the dolls." Jennifer heard her voice tremble.

"Maybe I did and maybe I didn't, and if I did maybe that better be a warning to some people who are a little too stuck up."

"I am not stuck up," Jennifer said.

"You ran off like I had leprosy," said Lizzie. "Telling me you'll babysit me some time. I could bust your face for that."

"I said that before I saw you. From the way your grandma talked I thought you were a baby, and from the way *you* talk I think you are."

"You better watch out, smarty." Lizzie blew a big bubble and looked very mean over it.

"*You* better watch out. I'll tell your grandmother about you." After she said this, Jennifer realized that if she told Mrs. McBride, the secret of the dolls was out. In fact, Lizzie had spoiled it anyway.

"You tell my grandma, and I'll get you," Lizzie said, making a fist and holding it up threateningly.

Jennifer, who was usually timid, amazed her-

self. "Well, here I am," she said. "Get me now, don't stand there blabbing."

Lizzie started coming closer, moving slowly with her chin thrust forward and one hand on her hip. Her glasses were smoking up. "You don't know what you're starting, you stupid nitwit. I happen to be Black Belt in Judo."

"Show me," Jennifer said. She knew the dolls were watching. "Come on, Black Belt, do your stuff."

Lizzie's face glowed like a fluorescent apple. She shoved it right up to Jennifer's and then, surprisingly, turned on her heels and stormed out the door. "I could kill you with the middle finger of my left hand," she shouted. "It wouldn't be a fair fight."

"Coward," Jennifer called after her.

The house seemed very quiet. Jennifer was too upset to play with the dolls. She went home and watched her father dye a tub full of lamb's wool a deep magenta. Then she went out to the barn and helped her mother by sanding the excess rough clay from the bottom of three planters which had just been fired. No matter what she did, her thoughts kept busy with Lizzie McBride. She decided Lizzie was another nasty piece of bad luck come to ruin the best thing that had happened to her in the country.

She couldn't get Lizzie the Terrible out of

her thoughts, even the next afternoon when she set off to the playhouse. She went over their fight in her mind. "Black Belt in Judo," she said out loud. "Black Belt in Stupidity, that's what she's got." She was still thinking about Lizzie McBride when Lizzie appeared in the narrow path just ahead.

"Well, here comes Miss Stuck-Up, going to play with her dollies."

"Why don't you just do everybody a favor and go back to the city?" Jennifer said furiously.

They stood still, facing each other, when to Jennifer's surprise Lizzie bent her head and seemed to deflate like a limp balloon. "I can't," she said. "For private reasons." She became sullen. "I'd go back in a minute if I could. How do you stand it up here?"

"I like it," said Jennifer. "I get to be alone, or at least I *used* to get to be alone."

"You mean in that stupid dolly house?"

"It isn't stupid. It was a secret place."

"No fooling," Lizzie said with interest. "You

mean you're the only one who knows about it?"

Jennifer nodded. "Until you showed up."

"Who cares about a bunch of dumb dollies, secret or no secret?" Lizzie laughed. "Dolls are stupid."

"Not these dolls," Jennifer replied very seriously. She had to be careful of how much she told Lizzie. She decided she could share the fact that the dolls were secret, but she would never tell about their talking. "These dolls are different. They're strange and valuable."

"Dolls are dolls," Lizzie said.

They started walking along together toward the clearing where the house stood. Jennifer wished Lizzie would turn around and go home, but she followed her right into the house.

They stood in the middle of the room and looked at the dolls. Lizzie seemed very intense.

"Yesterday, when you came, I had them in the middle of a ball," Jennifer said slowly. "I was about to serve the wine."

"I'll watch," said Lizzie.

Jennifer poured out wine and served it.

Lizzie said that the Princess doll looked like Eliza Doolittle, the girl in a movie she had seen. She told Jennifer the story and then started to use the dolls as actors. Before long each doll had been given the part of one of the characters in the movie. Lizzie was very good at making grand speeches for the dolls. She had memorized whole scenes from movies and shows.

It seemed no time had passed when the air was beginning to cool and the sun to go down. "It's late," said Lizzie. "Grandma's nervous when I'm around, but she's even more nervous if I'm away too long." She paused. "The reason I can't go back to the city—since you asked me before—is, they don't want me around. My folks say I'll just fool around and get into trouble. So they send me up here, where grandma can keep an eye on me. Who keeps an eye on you?"

"My folks," said Jennifer, "but they've got a lot on their minds right now."

"Trouble?"

Jennifer nodded. "Money trouble."

"You mean you're poor?" said Lizzie.

"I suppose so," said Jennifer, who never felt poor herself, but knew it described what they were.

Lizzie was thoughtful. They had closed the door of the doll house and were walking single file down the overgrown path that led to the gravel road. When they reached the road, Lizzie said seriously, "I'm very good at making money. Once I set up a toy exchange on my stoop. I made twenty bucks and bought myself a bike."

"My father needs more than that to pay the bank," said Jennifer.

"Of course, you couldn't set up a business here. Nobody'd come to a place like this, unless you had something really fantastic."

They kept walking in silence. Then suddenly Lizzie stopped. "But we do!" she shouted.

"We do what?" said Jennifer.

"We do have something fantastic. We have the dolls."

"We can't sell them." Jennifer was horrified. "They don't belong to us."

"But we can show them," said Lizzie. "We can exhibit them. We can make a museum."

Jennifer stared open-mouthed at her. "But they're our secret."

"I know, I know." Lizzie nodded her head. "And I'll never tell a soul unless you say it's okay, but what with your folks being poor and needing money . . ." She scowled. "Oh, forget it." She continued to walk.

Jennifer followed her in silence. "How much do you think we could make?" she said after a few minutes.

"No telling," said Lizzie. "A thing like that could be terrific or it could be a flop. It all depends on publicity and how word of mouth works. But I tell you one thing. My class went to a museum down in New York and they had two floors in it with nothing but dolls, and those dolls looked just like these dolls, and that place was packed."

"I know that museum," said Jennifer, "and you can get into it for nothing."

"So what? That's New York, where there

are sixty billion things to do. Up here in the sticks they'd pay through the old nose. Anyway, you don't like the idea, so forget it."

Soon they were at Mrs. McBride's gate. They made plans to meet at the playhouse in the morning.

Lizzie McBride, with her quick tricky ideas, had an odd effect on Jennifer. By the time she walked into the kitchen she knew that there would be a doll museum and that this had turned into a very unusual summer.

9

At breakfast the next morning Jennifer had a desire to tell her parents that she and Lizzie McBride had a plan that would make things better for them, but she knew that if she told them the plan they would say that it was wrong to make money out of somebody else's things. She worried about this herself and decided to talk to Lizzie about it.

"How do we make a museum?" said Jennifer to Lizzie when they met at the playhouse.

Lizzie put on a serious face. "You've got to set it up interesting, and you've got to advertise."

"Advertise?"

"We need posters on the road."

"My parents did that and a fat lot of good it did them," said Jennifer.

"No, dummy. I saw your folks' sign, it's mostly stuck behind branches. In the fall my grandma sells her apples off the road. I help her put up her signs. Lots of them, not one behind a tree. They say, 'Slow Down Fresh Apples Ahead' and 'A Thousand Yards to Fresh-Picked Juicy Apples,' stuff like that."

"But the doll museum isn't on the road. How will we get people to it?"

Lizzie took off her glasses and closed her eyes. "I don't know. . . . Yes, I do. We'll have to lead them in from the main road. That may add to the excitement. We could say it's a hidden secret museum of rare dolls."

"Forgotten dolls," said Jennifer.

"The Museum of the Forgotten Dolls. Admission twenty-five cents."

Jennifer thought of the signs. She could just see them up there on the road leading from the village. Anybody heading out of the A&P would see them. They could get the people who'd come off the thruway, and the summer cottage people too. The girls decided to use the back sides of Mrs. McBride's apple posters for signs.

When they went inside the playhouse they looked at it critically, trying to see it as a museum. "We've got to get it into shape," Lizzie said.

It needed a lot of fixing. Some of the boards would have to be replaced. The high grass around the house needed cutting, the house could use a coat of paint, and the dolls themselves needed to be put in more interesting positions.

"We're planning a lot of remodeling, Lizzie, and this isn't our place." Jennifer blurted out her worry.

Lizzie took off her glasses. "True," she said, "it's a risk, but if the old bird who owned them had cared she'd have fixed things up a long time ago. We care."

Jennifer's problem hadn't been solved, of course, but Lizzie made what they were planning sound right.

They found some white paint in Mrs. Mc-

Bride's garage and, in the back of the Fairfax barn, lumber which had been left over from the remodeling. They lugged their tools and materials out to the playhouse in Jennifer's rusty wagon, Mrs. McBride peering after them from the screen porch.

Lizzie did the woodwork, replacing the old porch boards while Jennifer slapped paint over the shingles. Lizzie had a fierce angry way of hammering that sometimes surprised Jennifer and made her laugh. While she worked Lizzie told Jennifer that she planned to be a doctor when she got older and would never get married. The next minute she'd say she would go out to Hollywood and be in TV shows or make movies or adopt ten children. She told Jennifer she was tough enough to handle anything because in the school she went to she got beaten up every afternoon.

"Every afternoon?" Jennifer said in amazement.

"Unless I give out candy or gum like a bribe."

"Why do they beat you?"

"Because I'm smart," said Lizzie. "Smart and fresh, and they're a bunch of eeediots, like just about everybody else."

"Including me?" said Jennifer.

"No, not including you." Lizzie banged a board so hard Jennifer thought the roof would come down.

"If you're so smart," Jennifer said slowly, "why don't you pretend to be dumb? Then they wouldn't bother you."

Lizzie put her hammer down and Jennifer wondered if she was thinking of punching her. Finally she tapped the hammer. "That's an idea," she said. "Maybe I'll use it and maybe I won't. What are you going to be?"

Jennifer had never told anyone her thoughts on that subject and so she was surprised to hear herself say, "An artist. I want to be a painter."

"That's good," said Lizzie. "I'll buy your paintings, if they're any good." She put down her hammer. "Hey, I think the old place is shaping up."

"Isn't twenty-five cents kind of high?" said

Jennifer. She had no idea of what people would spend and wondered if it wasn't nervy to charge money to see something she had found for nothing.

"You put a lot of work into it, right?" Lizzie said. "And a lot of thinking about it."

"I guess so," Jennifer said.

"Okay, that's worth something."

"I hope so," said Jennifer. She certainly had worked. Her arms ached from painting the walls of the house and she had one still to go. They would make the posters the next day. It was sundown. Time to go home.

"Where've you two been all day?" Mrs. McBride called to them from the fence. "I hope you're not up to any trouble, Miss Lizzie the Terrible."

Lizzie snarled and her grandmother smiled delightedly.

"Sure is good to see you out of the house. You look a different girl."

"Can Jennifer have supper with us, Grandma?"

"I don't know why not," said Mrs. McBride. "Call your mom and check if it's okay, Jennifer."

It was okay. Jennifer went up to wash with Lizzie and then came down to help set the table. Mrs. McBride was a wonderful cook. She made her own bread and enough food for twice the number of people she had to feed. There was only herself and Mr. McBride and Lizzie. Mr. McBride spent most of his day on the porch. Moving about on his two canes was painful to him. He read books or watched TV or talked to Lizzie or Mrs. McBride, or looked at his small garden. He liked to tell stories about the Mansion when it was full of people. He remembered how the gardens looked and what the parties were like.

Mrs. McBride served a lamb stew with potatoes and fresh peas. "I think it's a miracle that's come over Miss Lizzie," she said. "Two days ago you were a hollering horrible kid, and now you're a pleasure. What are you two up to?"

"We just like to play around near the big

house," said Jennifer. "There's so much to look at." She didn't like to lie, but what she said was certainly true, only not complete.

"There's no harm in that," Mrs. McBride said. "I'm glad that place is being put to some use. It's a pity to let a big beautiful house stand empty for all these years. It's wrong to let a house die. It's bad luck for everybody around it."

Jennifer thought Mrs. McBride was referring to her parents. "My father says we've had a run of bad luck and we're hoping for some of the other kind now."

"You don't wait around for good luck," said Mr. McBride, "you make it yourself. Arthritis got me crippled, but I call it good luck."

"I never said you weren't crazy," said Mrs. McBride.

"No, I am lucky to be able to sit still reading and looking around and talking to people. If I wasn't in my chair, there are a lot of books I'd never have read and a lot of thoughts I'd never have thought. You make your own luck and that's the truth. You can tell that to your folks, Jennifer." He winked at her.

Jennifer looked down at her plate. She didn't wish to discuss her parents' worries, but she wished her mother and father could take on some of Mr. McBride's positive point of view.

After dinner Lizzie took Jennifer up to her room to show her a few of the things she'd brought from New York. There were some comics, a jump rope, jacks, and a bag of marbles. They played jacks until it was time for Jennifer to go home. As they came downstairs Mrs. McBride called to them.

"Come in here, girls, there's something I want to talk to you about." The tone of her voice was so serious that it made Jennifer and Lizzie start.

"I just went out back to the garage, ladies." Mrs. McBride put her hands on her hips. "All my apple poster boards are missing, and a lot of paint, too. Now, I don't know what you two are up to. You told me you were just playing over at the big house, but I'll ask you to remem-

ber that the Needham property belongs to the Needhams, and though we often take walks in there and pick the berries and even take flowers and cuttings from the plants, that place is not anybody's but the Needhams'. So don't get any fancy notions."

Jennifer and Lizzie nodded their heads and stared at the rug. Their notion was just about as fancy as a notion could get and they both knew it.

10

When Jennifer got home, her parents were sitting over coffee at the kitchen table. They were talking excitedly.

"Jenny," said Beatrice Fairfax, "Mr. Duncan in town has offered us a corner of his shop. He says we can display our crafts and sell them from his store on a commission basis."

"A commission?" said Jennifer.

"He'll take a percentage of what we sell, and the rest is ours. It means that people will see our work."

"What's a percentage?" said Jennifer.

"If I sell a vase for five dollars, I give Mr. Duncan one dollar and keep the other four," said her mother.

Hugh Fairfax looked at his delighted wife and shook his head. "Four dollars, too little and too late to pay our bills and debts and keep us up here. I think we have to face up to the fact, Bea; store or no store, we've had a run of bad luck. I wouldn't be surprised if this turned out to be another disappointment."

"Why not make your own luck?" said Jennifer.

"What?" said her mother.

"Make your own luck," Jennifer repeated. "Don't wait for it to happen to you, make it happen."

Hugh Fairfax looked at his daughter sharply and then smiled. "That's what we're hoping to do in the store, Jenny," he said.

Jennifer went up to bed. Her mind was full of thoughts of the doll museum and the shop in town and the posters and Lizzie McBride and Mrs. McBride and how she had never had so much to think about before in her life, and she fell asleep.

Jennifer and Lizzie didn't discuss Mrs. Mc-

Bride's warning. They worked quietly the next day, only stopping for lunch. They ate inside the house because the sun was so strong. After lunch Lizzie went down to the lake for water to wash the floors. Jennifer realized that it had been a long time since she had been alone with the dolls.

Just then the Queen doll said, "You don't play with us at all. Only that one day you played with us."

"We're fixing the house now," said Jennifer. "We're going to make it into a museum where people can come and admire you."

"I'd rather be played with," said the Princess.

"I don't mind being looked at," said the Queen, "now that I'm beautiful."

"But we wish you'd play with us again," said the Jester. "You know, make up funny things for me to do, the way you did the other day."

"We will play with you," Jennifer promised.

When Lizzie came back they did the floors

and then sat down to write the posters. One said FANTASTIC MUSEUM FULL OF RARE OLD DOLLS . . . 25 CENTS. Another said SLOW DOWN REST YOURSELF ENJOY ANTIQUE DOLLS. Underneath it said SPECIAL GUIDE WILL LEAD YOU TO MUSEUM. Another said STOP HERE FOR A WALK THROUGH THE MUSEUM IN THE WILD. Lizzie wrote that one. Jennifer didn't like it.

"It isn't wild," she said. "That sounds like a jungle."

"It is a jungle, as a matter of fact," Lizzie said.

"It is not. It's overgrown weeds."

"That sounds stupid. THE DOLL MUSEUM IN THE OVERGROWN WEEDS."

They were silent for a few minutes, and Lizzie changed WILD to WOOD.

Inside the house they found an old end table which they painted and put near the door. They placed a stool beside it. "This is our admission booth," Lizzie said.

At the end of the day they stood in front of the house and looked at it hard. "It still isn't right," said Lizzie. "It's missing something. It doesn't look like a museum."

"What makes a museum look like a museum, and not other places?" said Jennifer. "Once when we lived down in the city my school took us to a big beautiful old house and on it it said THE FRICK COLLECTION. I asked my teacher if that meant it was a collection of Fricks. She said it was their paintings. They made their house into a museum."

"What if we wrote THE DOLL MUSEUM on top of the roof," said Lizzie, "in very big letters."

"THE MUSEUM OF THE FORGOTTEN DOLLS," said Jennifer.

"We can't fit that in," said Lizzie.

"Yes, we can," Jennifer insisted. "Your grandma's got three cans of red paint."

It took two days to paint the sign on the roof and scythe the high grass down. Finally they were ready for opening day.

On a Thursday morning they set out with the posters and nails and a hammer. In the corner of each poster they had written the opening date as well as the words, "Proprietors, Jennifer Fairfax and Lizzie McBride."

After all the posters were up, they checked on the museum. They tried many different arrangements of the dolls. Jennifer put the Queen at one end of the table, the King at the other. She had the Jester doing a handstand next to the King and all the other dolls watching him perform. She put the Baby doll next to

the Queen, holding a tray on which some cups
were arranged. She managed to get the Princess
to hold a teacup as if she were waiting for it to
be filled. She wiped their faces and dusted the
room. Lizzie washed the china and oiled the
table. And then it was time to go.

Birds shrilled; the country was thick with them, darting and soaring. Crickets and bees had set up their own racket for the setting sun. Everything was green and soft. A sudden night breeze came on.

Beatrice Fairfax stood at the kitchen sink washing her hands. She looked upset. "I can't get anything right today," she said. "The glazes won't set right, I keep getting air bubbles in the clay. Now that we have a store interested in our work, everything starts to go wrong." She suddenly turned on Jennifer. "And what's this about a doll museum? Is the proprietor by any chance the Jennifer Fairfax who resides at this address?"

"It is," said Jennifer. She was glad her mother finally knew about the museum.

"For heaven's sake, but you're the secretive one," her mother exclaimed. "Is that what you and the McBride girl have been so busy at? Mrs. McBride was dancing a jig out of curiosity."

"We're in business," said Jennifer. "We

open tomorrow and we're going to make a lot of money. Maybe enough to pay the bank."

"That," said Beatrice Fairfax harshly, "is just pie-in-the-sky nonsense. I am surprised to hear it coming from you, Jennifer Fairfax. You were our practical one. Now you sound as silly as your mother and father. I thought that watching us would give you a little more sense." Her eyes filled with tears. "Don't you see how foolish it is to think you can take your dreams and make them work? Don't say I didn't warn you."

"But we've planned it all out very carefully," said Jennifer. "And we've worked very hard and we're going to have a success." She started up the stairs.

"By the way," her mother called, "where did these dolls come from?"

"I found them at the Needham place, all forgotten in an old forgotten playhouse."

"Just a minute, Jennifer." Beatrice Fairfax walked up the stairs toward Jennifer and put a hand on her shoulder. "You can't use Mrs.

Needham's dolls. Those aren't your dolls and that isn't your house."

"I'm not keeping them."

"You have to get permission."

"I will, I will, only please let us open the museum."

"All right," said Beatrice Fairfax, "but you'll promise to write her a letter in the morning."

"Yes," said Jennifer. "I promise."

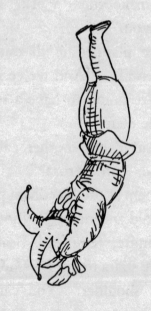

II

Jennifer didn't write the letter in the morning. They were much too busy. Mrs. McBride made a pitcher of punch and a batch of brownies for them to take over to the playhouse. Lizzie was busy putting up more signs with arrows pointing to the spot where the guide would take people to the hidden museum.

At eleven o'clock they were ready. Clifford Tillman, a boy who lived down the road, came with his two little sisters. Jennifer led them to the museum where Lizzie took their money, offered them brownies and punch, and showed them the room full of dolls. Then Jennifer raced back to the road to take the next customers to the museum.

There weren't exactly crowds of people waiting; in fact, there was mostly nobody on the road. Mrs. McBride came by, and so did the Fairfaxes.

Later in the afternoon Jennifer and Lizzie decided to finish the leftover punch and brownies and close up. As they were closing the door, Clifford Tillman walked up with his two little sisters and three of their friends. They said they didn't have any more money, but could they just peek in anyway? Lizzie said, "Okay, but don't make a habit of it."

After they closed up, Lizzie and Jennifer counted their money. One dollar and fifty cents.

"This is nothing but chicken feed," Lizzie scowled, "and we need mortgage money, for Pete's sake."

Jennifer thought of her parents' high hopes and bad luck. "We can't charge more, that's for sure," she said.

"Not unless we offer more," said Lizzie.

Jennifer stared at the dolls, thinking hard.

To her surprise they seemed to be looking back at her, with a silent clear message in their gaze.

"We *can* offer more," Jennifer cried. "We can play with them. Put on special plays, like Cinderella or the Sleeping Beauty. We could make shows."

Lizzie had to think seriously about an idea that wasn't her own. So she gave a few minutes to silent staring before she said, "Good idea, good idea. Every afternoon at two o'clock we put on a play. But we have to do a smash-bang job of advertising it."

"Can't we just write it down on the old posters?" said Jennifer, who was exhausted.

They painted the information about shows every afternoon into the corners of the posters. Lizzie said they needed to think up more ways to spread the word. Finally, tired and depressed, they dragged their feet home.

"And now, perhaps you've learned the lesson your father and I have been learning," said Beatrice Fairfax at supper. "Nothing is easy."

Jennifer stared at her plate.

"And that letter to Mrs. Needham gets written tonight, if I have to write it myself," her mother concluded.

When the supper dishes had been cleared, Jennifer sat down at the table to work on the letter. First she worked out a scratch copy on a yellow pad and then copied it in her neatest and clearest script onto a piece of white stationery with blue lines crossing it and bunches of flowers at the top. She spent one hour working on the letter. When she was finished, Mrs. Fairfax called the postmistress at home and got Mrs. Needham's city address. The letter was stamped and addressed and placed in the letter box with the red flag up.

It was time for bed. Jennifer felt a knot of worry take over her thoughts. Nothing good could come of that letter, she thought. It would bring to an end the most exciting summer of her life.

12

No one came the next day. Jennifer and Lizzie closed the museum early. It was too hot, and since there was no business at all, they went for a swim.

Jennifer said, "My mother was right. Daydreams don't work out. Pie-in-the-sky daydreams fall flat when you try to make them real."

Lizzie floated on her back, her best position for getting ideas. She said, "Advertise, advertise, that's what we need to do."

"How about a TV commercial?" Jennifer said dismally.

Lizzie flipped over and spat water out. "No,

but the newspaper. Why didn't I think of it before?" She got so excited that she ran out of the water and grabbed up her clothes, not bothering to dry.

"Where are you going?" Jennifer called after her.

"To put an ad in that hick newspaper, dummy."

"It'll cost money," said Jennifer. "It may cost everything we've made."

"Think big," Lizzie said, and ran toward the path.

Jennifer followed her slowly.

They went back to the McBrides' and phoned the newspaper to place the ad. It said, "Come see Rare Antique Dolls in Hidden Museum Perform Favorite Old Fairy Tales and Original Plays." The ad cost one dollar and fifteen cents.

The next day it rained. It rained as if to make up for all the days of the summer that had been sunny and clear. Their spirits as gray as the sky, Jennifer and Lizzie couldn't decide whether to bother to open the museum or not. Who would ever come out on a day like that?

As it turned out, more than thirty children and adults. The cars were lined up on the road. They had read the newspaper ad on that rainy morning. Rain meant the children couldn't swim or bike, and so they were happy to come to the museum. Coins filled the money box.

At two o'clock Lizzie and Jennifer moved the table to the wall where it could serve as a stage and left the room open for the audience to sit on the floor. There were twelve children and three mothers. "Today, we the Museum Players present the story of Little Red Riding Hood," said Lizzie, standing before the group.

They used the Princess for Red Riding Hood and the Queen and Jester for Grandmother and Wolf. Jennifer worked Red Riding Hood. Lizzie did the Grandmother and Wolf. Jennifer and Lizzie moved the dolls and changed their voices to suit the drama. The dolls were so beautiful and so gracefully made that it was a delight to watch them. At the end

of the show, there were refreshments provided by Mrs. McBride.

Jennifer opened the door of the playhouse so the young audience could file out. The rain had stopped. A thin sun shone in the gray sky and the air was keen and fresh and fragrant.

When everyone had gone Jennifer and Lizzie counted eight dollars and fifty cents.

"Chicken feed?" said Jennifer.

"Nope," said Lizzie. "Mortgage money."

Lizzie took some posters over to the roadside fruit stand nearest to them while Jennifer stayed to tidy up the playhouse and get it ready for the next day.

"Now, are you pleased?" she said when Lizzie had gone. "They admire you and we play with you. I've written to Mrs. Needham for permission."

"It is good fun," said the King, "but you didn't give me a big part. I don't consider the Huntsman a leading role, my dear, even if he is very brave."

"On Monday you will play the Prince in Cinderella," Jennifer promised.

"Very well," said the King. "Now, who is Mrs. Needham?"

"Why, she's the lady who owns you."

"She's the one who left us to rot, you mean," said the Queen. "She was a nasty spoiled little girl."

"Was she?" Jennifer was alarmed.

"Now, my dear lady," the Jester admonished the Queen. "She wasn't that bad, you know. She had a temper and she was spoiled, but that's not unusual. She did hug me quite a lot."

"Hug you till you crunch," said the Princess. "I loathed her. She was mean to us and to her friends. She ordered everybody about all the time and insisted she was the best and the prettiest. She wanted everything to be perfect. Why, if one of us got a spot on our clothes she'd as soon set us aside and ask her grandpa for a new doll."

"Thank goodness for that," said the Peasant doll, "or her grandpa wouldn't have supplied her with all of us. We might have been left on the store shelf."

"And would that have been worse than being left by her?" the Baby doll pouted. "She came here once after she grew up. Remember? She was with her husband. She wanted to show us off. She laughed at us because we were so untidy."

The other dolls lowered their gaze with the painful recollection.

"It's true," said the King. "I had forgotten, dear. She laughed at us and called us 'that heap of wax I passed my childhood among.' Then she closed the door and that was the last time we saw a living soul till you came, Jennifer." He looked at Jennifer. "And now you've asked her permission. I can't think her answer will please you."

"I had to do it," Jennifer said.

With a heavy heart she finished tidying the house and bid them good-bye.

13

The next morning Jennifer slept late. She was awakened by the telephone's ring and then her mother's voice calling, "It's for you Jennifer, long distance." She ran downstairs, and took the phone from her mother, who smiled encouragingly at her.

"Hello," said Jennifer.

A thin scratching voice, which sounded as if it came from a distance over water and hills, answered. "Hello. This is Kathleen Needham. Am I speaking with Miss Jennifer Fairfax?"

"Yes," said Jennifer.

The voice grew louder. It was unpleasant. "I have received your letter this morning, Miss

Fairfax. It appears that you are asking my permission for something you have already taken it upon yourself to do without my permission. Am I correct?"

"I—I—yes," Jennifer stammered.

"The time to ask permission is before you do a thing, child, not after. Are you not aware of that?"

Jennifer said that she was, but the voice drove on.

"Then you are a very tricky little girl, and I don't approve of tricky children."

Jennifer felt ill in her empty stomach.

"I do not remember your mother or your father, and I had entirely forgotten about my old playhouse. If I had remembered I would certainly have taken those precious dolls out of there years ago. Now, see here. I've not been up to the house for quite a time, but I intend to come up now. I want to find out exactly what's going on. So good-bye to you, and my advice is, be less tricky in the future, if you please."

Jennifer was about to say that she would, but the phone clicked on the other end and she whispered her good-bye to a dead receiver. A lump of misery filled her chest and seemed to swell like a balloon to fill her entire self.

"Now," said Beatrice Fairfax, "did she give her permission?"

"No," said Jennifer, "she didn't."

"Did she tell you you had to stop the museum?"

"No," said Jennifer, "she didn't."

"Then cheer up," said Beatrice Fairfax, surprisingly. "If she didn't say yes, she didn't say no either."

"Do you think we could?"

"Keep it up," said her mother, "until she tells you 'No.' Now stop looking like the end of the world and have some breakfast." She poured out a glass of milk and set it on the table, then drew up Jennifer's chin with her hand. "I'd like to bring some cookies and juice over for your audience this afternoon," she said. "I'll bet you get a big crowd."

Down in New York City, Mrs. Kathleen Needham sat beside her telephone, tapping a pencil nervously on her desk. She was a large woman who felt small and helpless. All her life, and especially since her husband's death, everybody had done things for her. Maids did her housework, chauffeurs drove her car. Lawyers tended to her business. There wasn't much left for her to do but be cross with the way they did things. She had no interest in the world outside her own household.

She liked everything and everyone to be perfect. Therefore she had only one friend. This friend, a Miss Maroony, wore a hearing aid, and whenever Mrs. Needham started to complain, she simply switched her hearing off. Sometimes they went to the ballet or shopping; mostly Miss Maroony sat and did not listen while Mrs. Needham grumbled. She grumbled about things not being tidy enough. Was that dress really cleaned properly? Ought those papers to have been signed? Did the tires really have to be changed, or was everyone taking advantage of her and spending her money recklessly?

When the maid had brought her the mail

that very morning, she also brought a breakfast tray. On the tray was a pitcher of coffee,
a cup, and an egg. The egg was overdone by
Mrs. Needham's standards. Mrs. Needham
fired the cook. Then she opened Jennifer's
letter.

When she read it, it seemed to her that one

more person was taking advantage of her. She planned to do something about it. She decided she would personally take care of the situation. She would do it without help from lawyers or maids or anyone. She was going to tell Harry, her chauffeur, to drive her up to the old house so that she could investigate.

She couldn't remember when she had been so excited.

Jennifer told Lizzie McBride about the telephone call. The two girls were so unhappy about what it meant that they were hardly aware of the fine business the museum did that morning. The posters Lizzie had put up at the roadside stand had brought in people from a campsite nearby. The girls were, however, surprised to see Mrs. McBride huffing and puffing through the clearing.

"Grandma, what are you doing here?" said Lizzie.

"I had a telephone call I thought might interest you," said Mrs. McBride, patting her wet forehead. "Mrs. Needham called me this morning and told me she's coming up tomorrow noon. I'm to get the gatehouse open and serve her a lunch. Can you just imagine that? Telling me to open that old house and clean it and make it ready to serve her a lunch. She must think she's the Queen of England and I'm Wonder Woman." Mrs. McBride was red with indignation.

Jennifer and Lizzie were alarmed. Even the dolls seemed to grow pensive. The day went by very slowly. They put on Snow White for a small group of children but were too distracted to do a good job, and the audience seemed to lose interest.

When they were closing up the museum and counting their money, Jennifer realized she was not paying attention and kept making mistakes. In the short time since she had found the house, so many new things had happened to her. To go back to the way things were before was something she could not bear to think about. She had made a strange new friend. She had rescued the dolls from their misery. She had started a museum. Now Mrs. Needham was coming to ruin everything.

They hung a Museum Closed sign on the door and slowly picked their way down to the lake for a swim. Lizzie floated on her back and stared at the sky. "Well," she said, "what's our plan?"

"We don't have one," said Jennifer.

"Then let's get one, for Pete's sake. What do we say to the old girl?"

Jennifer was horrified to hear Mrs. Needham referred to that way. "We show her the museum and ask her permission and she'll say NO."

Lizzie flipped over and ducked her head under the water. When she came up she shook her head fiercely. "Why don't we make a big fuss over her? You know, 'Oh Dear Good and Gracious Lady, we present a special play in your honor!'"

Jennifer treaded water. "How about songs and dances in her honor, too?"

"And poems and dinners and lunches."

"And mugs and rugs."

They splashed and cooled off, and put their clothes on and walked home . . . without a plan.

14

The next day was chilly, a forerunner of the fall. Gray clouds massed over the meadows and hills and blocked the sunlight. The air was heavy and damp. The day expressed Jennifer's feelings exactly.

At home, her parents were excited. Beatrice Fairfax was excited about a set of salad bowls she'd been asked to make; Hugh Fairfax was excited about a new rug that he had been commissioned to weave. Jennifer couldn't stand her parents' good cheer. She left the house in the middle of the morning to walk over to Lizzie's.

Lizzie and Jennifer played jacks halfheartedly and then watched TV and then talked to Mr. McBride. Mrs. McBride was busy with

Mrs. Lane over at the gatehouse, cleaning and preparing lunch. The day was no longer chilly, but growing hot and muggy. At noon the Mc-Brides' dog began to yap, and Mr. McBride hobbled to the front porch and raised a hand over his eyes.

"Well, there she blows," he said.

The two girls ran out onto the porch and looked over at the gatehouse where a long black Rolls had pulled up. A uniformed chauffeur held the door open for a large woman in a white and blue flowered dress. One of her white-gloved hands held onto the chauffeur's arm, the other held a small straw hat and a white straw purse.

The woman stood up and took a deep breath, looking around her critically. She had very white hair and a strong face with a surprisingly nervous expression on it. She looked almost angry and then seemed to relax. She turned to the steps of the gatehouse where Mrs. McBride and Mrs. Lane stood smiling uneasily, waiting to greet her. Mrs. McBride came halfway down the stairs, her hand thrust out to be shaken. As

Jennifer and Lizzie crossed the road they heard her say, "Welcome to you, Mrs. Needham, it's been a long time."

"Has it been?" said the woman in the high unpleasant voice Jennifer recognized from the telephone. "Perhaps it has. Things don't seem to stay the same, do they?" She reached the top step. "Has luncheon been prepared, Mrs. McBride? I'm very hungry. I do hope you've made some of your muffins, Mrs. Lane. I remember your excellent muffins." She glanced over at her chauffeur. "Oh, yes, and send a tray out for my chauffeur if you please." She strode into the house. Jennifer and Lizzie watched her disappear down the dark front hall. Mrs. McBride and Mrs. Lane followed her.

The two girls walked over to the Rolls. They had never been able to examine one close up before.

The chauffeur smiled at them and took off his hat. "Hot day," he said. "Want to see the inside?"

The girls nodded. He held the door open for them.

"Don't tell the old girl on me, now," he said as they climbed in.

"We won't," Lizzie said. His words were not comforting. Mrs. Needham was the sort of woman whose chauffeur had to do kind things behind her back. The girls settled into the cool leather of the back seat. "It's no pickup truck, I'll tell you that much," Lizzie whispered.

The door to the gatehouse opened. Mrs. McBride, glistening and red-faced, bustled out, bearing a tray of sandwiches and beer for the chauffeur. She poked her serious face into the window of the car. "Mrs. N. wants to see you two now."

They left the car slowly. In spite of the heat of the day, Jennifer's hands were icy.

Mrs. Needham did not look up when the girls entered the dining room. She was cutting a slice of ham. After she cut it she took a cube of it on her fork and put it in her mouth. Then she chewed it slowly for quite a while before she swallowed it. Finally she looked up at them.

"Which of you is Jennifer Fairfax?" she said.

"I am, and how do you do?" said Jennifer.

"Speak up, please," said Mrs. Needham. "I don't read lips."

"Yes, Mrs. Needham."

"After lunch you will go with me to my old playhouse, and then we shall discuss this museum you've made out of it without permission of any kind."

"Yes, Mrs. Needham," said Jennifer.

"Wait for me outside. I don't like people watching me eat." She began to slice the ham again and the girls thankfully departed. Even Lizzie was subdued by Mrs. Needham.

They sat on the steps of the gatehouse and watched Harry Tomac, the chauffeur, eat his lunch. He told them how peculiar Mrs. Needham was. "She's alone so much," he said. "It makes her eccentric. Deep down I think she's afraid of people."

"She's pretty frightening," Jennifer said.

The door opened behind them and Mrs. Needham stood uncertainly on the threshold.

"Well now, come along. It's time to go," she said. "Harry, will you join us?" It was not a question, but an order. Harry jumped to his feet.

Jennifer led the silent group down the gravel road. Mrs. Needham looked over at the Mansion and her eyes clouded. "Well, there it is," she said to no one in particular. "It's been so many years, it doesn't hurt me to see it now. It really doesn't. That's time for you."

They turned down the path to the lake. "Incidentally, I do remember your mother," she said to Jennifer. "She was a very pretty and helpful young woman. Very talented, as I remember. You look something like her, Miss Fairfax."

"Thank you," said Jennifer.

"Two fine young ladies," Harry said encouragingly. But Mrs. Needham kept silent.

They walked down the bramble path which had been widened by all the traffic on it over the last few days. It was still difficult for Mrs. Needham to manage without snagging her stockings. Harry had to hold the twigs apart for her to pass, and she objected to the thorns. "No wonder I stopped going to that old house," she said bitterly. "Only a child or an idiot would want to get to it."

Finally they reached the clearing. Jennifer remembered the first time she had seen the house and the surprise of its being there came over her again. She half feared that the dolls would be as she had found them the first time and that everything else had been a dream.

15

But when they opened the door the dolls were as clean and orderly as when they had left them. They sat up straight in their chairs, reflecting the expectancy of the people in the room.

Harry said, "What beautiful little dollies."

"Why, they're just as I left them," said Mrs. Needham. "Of course, I remember exactly. What do you mean by saying you saved them from being ruined? You haven't. Aren't they lovely." She stood gazing at them quite lost in thought. The room was very still.

"Mrs. Needham," said Jennifer, "we would like to put on an original play for you, in your honor, so you can see for yourself how we run our shows."

Lizzie looked stupefied. "An original play?" she said.

Jennifer nodded. She felt quite sure of what she was doing, but at the same time surprised at herself for doing it, since it was always Lizzie who had the good ideas. "It's the one about the girl who finds an abandoned doll house filled with sad forgotten dolls," she said.

"Oh, yeah," Lizzie said. "That one." She rolled her eyes to the ceiling so that only Jennifer could see her.

"Do handle them carefully and don't make it too long," said Mrs. Needham. "Don't get carried away, I have very little patience." She sat down awkwardly on one of the low chairs while Harry straddled another.

Jennifer and Lizzie put the table into position to serve as a stage and gathered the dolls to one side of it. Jennifer chose one of the numerous girl dolls, walked her across the table, and spoke for her: "I'm so lost! I've been picking berries,

turning this way and that, and now I've no idea how to get home. How dark it's getting, and how thick the wood gets! But wait, someone is crying."

Lizzie made a sound of forlorn crying. Jennifer was relieved that Lizzie had gotten the idea of the story and was throwing herself into it with her usual intensity.

"And there, what do I see," she went on. "It's a little house, a little ruin of a house in the middle of a clearing, and the crying is coming from the house." Lizzie increased the crying to a howl.

Jennifer walked the doll along the table and had her open an imaginary door and look at all the dolls grouped behind it in an imaginary room. She had her doll describe the room, its filth and misery, and then the incredible moment when the dolls began to speak. Mrs. Needham began to fidget during the dolls' description of how they had been left to rot, but when Jennifer had her girl return after cleaning the dolls to find them messed again, she grew still and interested.

Lizzie spoke for one of the dolls: "The girl who came and messed us up was a mean nasty creep. She threw us around and knocked our heads and we hate her. She's a villain."

Jennifer answered, speaking for the girl, "I'll find her and make her answer for this."

"Help! There she is!" cried Lizzie.

Lizzie and Jennifer acted out their first fight, to Mrs. Needham's pleasure. After the two enemies became friends and decided to make the playhouse into a museum where the dolls could be admired and enjoyed, Jennifer made a closing speech.

"We'll make believe with them, and we'll do it ourselves. It will be something of our own to do, without people bossing us and telling us," she said.

Mrs. Needham sat back with her hands in her lap as the dolls were bent forward from their waists in stiff bows. Jennifer and Lizzie smiled at Harry, who applauded loudly.

"Very interesting," said Mrs. Needham, "very interesting. So you think little girls can go around doing things for themselves without being told, eh? Without being bossed?"

Jennifer's heart sank.

"All I can say is, it's a fine idea, but I've never found a way to do it, and I'm an old lady. Anyway, you did things for yourselves by helping yourself to *my* dolls. I never gave permission and I'm not about to give away my property."

"We're not asking for it," said Jennifer. "We don't want any gifts from you."

"I should say not. That would be spoiling you, and spoiled children are what's wrong with everything now."

"We're in business, Mrs. Needham," said Lizzie. "We do things in a businesslike way. We would be happy to make you a partner."

"A what?" said Mrs. Needham sharply. "A what?"

"As we've said, we don't want any presents. We'll pay rent."

"Or you can take a percentage," said Jennifer. "We'll put it in writing if you like and we can all sign."

Mrs. Needham took a deep breath. Her

cheeks were pink under her powder. Her eyes grew moist and bird-bright. Her breath came short. She was very excited. She returned Lizzie's stare. "I'll take a flat rent," she said. "I like that idea."

In fact, she was delighted by it. She was doing her own business for her own self just as she had always dreamed. Even if it was with two ten-year-old girls over a playhouse, it couldn't have been more important to her if she had been dealing with the bank over the sale of the entire estate.

"We can pay five dollars a month," said Lizzie, "and we only want it for two months. Then we close down with Miss Fairfax looking after things during the winter."

"I'll take seven," said Mrs. Needham.

"We'll go no higher than six fifty," said Lizzie. "That's it."

"Very well," said Mrs. Needham. "Though I think it's a steal."

"These dolls are of no use to you, Mrs. Needham," said Lizzie.

"But they are to you," Mrs. Needham snapped. "Now, then, let's draw up the contract."

"I'll write it up," Lizzie said, "when we get back."

"I can sign before I leave," said Mrs. Needham. "I do so like to do my own business. I always knew I would have a gift for it."

They went back to the gatehouse. Mrs. Needham had Harry fetch pen and paper from the McBrides. Mrs. McBride was hanging over the front fence, her eyes popping with curiosity.

"There now," said Mrs. Needham, after she'd signed the contract with a flourish. "Harry will be our witness. Sign over there, Harry."

Harry signed. Jennifer signed. Lizzie signed.

"I expect my payment on the first of next month," said Mrs. Needham. "Don't forget or I shall have to send you a bill."

Harry helped her down the steps to her car and placed her inside it. She rolled down the window and beckoned to Mrs. McBride. "Thank you for lunch," she called. "Tell Mrs. Lane the muffins were excellent. This has been a most satisfying day, most satisfying." Then she turned to Jennifer and Lizzie. "You've rented the little house," she said, "but not the dolls."

The girls exchanged a worried look. Would they be charged an extra sum for the dolls?

"I'm giving the dolls to you," said Mrs. Needham. "They're yours." She turned abruptly and rolled up her window so as not to hear their thanks. Then she tapped the glass partition which separated her from Harry and he started the motor, with a side wink and tip of the cap.

16

"Hey there, you two," Mrs. McBride called from across the road. "What happened?"

They went up to the porch to tell the McBrides the story. When they'd finished, Mrs. McBride clapped a hand to her brow and laughed loudly. "That's a good business deal. You're sure a pair of fine bargainers."

"Hey, Sally," her husband said. "Why don't we celebrate the contract?"

"I've got enough food left over from Mrs. Needham's lunch to serve an army. She eats like a sick hummingbird," Mrs. McBride said enthusiastically. "Jennifer, I'm going to invite your folks and we're all going to celebrate."

Jennifer and Lizzie left Mrs. McBride with her party plans and took the path back through the woods.

"The story you made up, it was spooky," said Lizzie. "I never heard you act like that. You were like a professional."

"I know," Jennifer said. "I hardly even thought about it. It just happened. The story kept coming as if the dolls were making it up themselves. Talking through me."

Lizzie looked at her very seriously. "And me," she said.

The dolls were arranged as they had left them, only a feeling of deep contentment now filled the room. Lizzie and Jennifer dusted and tidied in silence. Both of them were too taken up with all the events of the day to speak much.

That evening Mr. and Mrs. Fairfax, Mr. and Mrs. McBride, Jennifer, and Lizzie sat down at the long wood table under Mr. McBride's lilac tree. They ate ham and beans and Mrs. Lane's muffins and drank chilled cider from a jug.

"These girls aren't the only ones who've had good news today," said Hugh Fairfax.

Beatrice Fairfax smiled. "Tell them, Hugh," she said.

"Your mother's work is selling very well," he said.

"When the salad bowls are finished I've got another commission for a set of plates," said Beatrice Fairfax unbelievingly.

"So we don't have to worry about the bank for now," Hugh Fairfax concluded.

"But we were making money for that out of our museum," said Jennifer. "We wanted to help."

"You did help, Jenny," said her father.

"No, I didn't," she protested. "Not yet."

"Oh, yes, you did," said her mother. "We watched you two go out with all that determination and spunk and try to do something, make it happen, and we began to realize how many things we hadn't tried. We were sitting there doing our work and expecting people to come to us on winds of good luck. You two made your own luck."

Looking out from under the lilac tree across the sloping lawn, over to the meadows and hills and deep woods of the Needham estate, Jennifer thought about the summer. There was her new friend Lizzie McBride and the museum they had made. There was her parents' new hope. And there were the amazing dolls who had started it all. Had they really spoken? Or was it something else, like the magic that had come to her that afternoon in a play she'd never planned to put on?

"What are you thinking about, Jennifer?" her mother said.

"Magic, I guess," she said.

Mr. McBride sighed. "Magic is when luck gets lucky."

"You better eat some more ham before you all fly off with the moths," said Mrs. McBride.

And they all did.

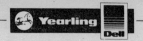